Welcome to ALADDIN QUIX!

If you are looking for fast, fun-to-read stories with colorful characters, lots of kid-friendly humor, easy-to-follow action, entertaining story lines, and lively illustrations, then **ALADDIN QUIX** is for you!

But wait, there's more!

If you're also looking for stories with tables of contents; word lists; about-the-book questions; 64, 80, or 96 pages; short chapters; short paragraphs; and large fonts, then **ALADDIN QUIX** is *definitely* for you!

ALADDIN QUIX: The next step between ready to reads and longer, more challenging chapter books, for readers five to eight years old.

Our Principal's in His Underwear!

Read more ALADDIN QUIX books!

By Stephanie Calmenson

Our Principal Is a Frog!
Our Principal Is a Wolf!
Our Principal's in His Underwear!

Royal Sweets
By Helen Perelman

Book 1: *A Royal Rescue*
Book 2: *Sugar Secrets*
Book 3: *Stolen Jewels*

A Miss Mallard Mystery
By Robert Quackenbush

Dig to Disaster
Texas Trail to Calamity
Express Train to Trouble
Stairway to Doom
Bicycle to Treachery
Gondola to Danger

★ Our Principal's ★
in His Underwear!

Previously titled *The Principal's New Clothes*

BY **Stephanie Calmenson**

ILLUSTRATED BY **Aaron Blecha**

ALADDIN QUIX

New York   London   Toronto   Sydney   New Delhi

ALADDIN QUIX
Simon & Schuster Children's Publishing Division
1230 Avenue of the Americas, New York, New York 10020
First Aladdin QUIX paperback edition January 2019
Text copyright © 1989 by Stephanie Calmenson
Illustrations copyright © 2019 by Aaron Blecha
The text of this work was previously published
as *The Principal's New Clothes* by Scholastic, Inc.
Also available in an Aladdin QUIX hardcover edition.
All rights reserved, including the right of reproduction in whole or in part in any form.
ALADDIN and the related marks and colophon
are trademarks of Simon & Schuster, Inc.
For information about special discounts for
bulk purchases, please contact Simon & Schuster Special Sales
at 1-866-506-1949 or business@simonandschuster.com.
The Simon & Schuster Speakers Bureau can bring authors to your live event. For more
information or to book an event contact the Simon & Schuster Speakers Bureau
at 1-866-248-3049 or visit our website at www.simonspeakers.com.
Cover designed by Karin Paprocki
Interior designed by Heather Palisi and Karin Paprocki
The illustrations for this book were rendered digitally.
The text of this book was set in Archer Medium.
Manufactured in the United States of America 1218 OFF
2 4 6 8 10 9 7 5 3 1
Library of Congress Control Number 2018956675
ISBN 978-1-4814-6672-1 (hc)
ISBN 978-1-4814-6671-4 (pbk)
ISBN 978-1-4814-6673-8 (eBook)

To you, my reader

—S. C.

Cast of Characters

Mr. Barnaby Bundy: Principal

Ms. Ivy Irving: Tailor and trickster

Mr. Moe Jackson: Tailor and trickster

Ms. Marilyn Moore: Assistant principal

Roger Patel: Top student and class leader

Mrs. Gwen Feeny: Third-grade teacher

Benny Shore: Coffee shop owner

Hector Gonzalez: Loves making his friends laugh

Nancy Wong: Hopes to be a zoologist

Alice Wright: Kindergartener who always tells the truth

Contents

Greetings, Mr. B!

Everyone at PS 88 knows that **Mr. Bundy** is the best principal in town. They also know that he's the sharpest dresser. That's why his students don't want to miss a day of school. They like to see what he's wearing.

One day, he'll have on a three-piece suit, with a crisply ironed handkerchief peeking out of his pocket.

The next day, it will be a snazzy plaid jacket, with matching tie and socks.

"Looking good, Mr. B!" his students always say.

Word got around about Mr. Bundy's clothes, and one day, a man and a woman who said they were **tailors** called on him.

They handed him their business card.

On one side the card said:

MOE & IVY

EXPERT TAILORS

And on the other side it said:

WE MAKE SUITS
THAT SUIT YOU FINE.

But they were not really tailors. They were **tricksters**.

"Greetings, Mr. B," said **Ivy**. "How would you like to buy an amazing, one-of-a-kind suit? That means no one but *you* will own it!"

"Thanks, but I don't think so," said Mr. Bundy. "I have so many suits already. I really don't need another."

"Ah, but this is no ordinary suit," said **Moe**. "It has special powers. *Very* special powers."

"What do you mean?" asked
Mr. Bundy.

Moe looked to his left.

He looked to his right.

Then he whispered in Mr. Bundy's ear, "We make our clothes from special cloth. It's invisible to anyone who's not good at his job or is a **nincompoop**."

"Really?" said Mr. Bundy. **"That's amazing!"**

"Yes," said Ivy. "You'll find out about everyone at your school while looking really **spiffy**."

"I do like to look spiffy," said Mr. Bundy.

Ivy didn't give him a chance to think another thought.

"Now, if you'll take off your jacket and lift up your arms, sir," said Ivy, grinning, "we will take your measurements."

"We will also take your money," mumbled Moe.

2

First Peek

The next day, Moe and Ivy set up a workshop in the gym. It was not long before the whole school heard about the amazing cloth and wanted to see it.

Students asked to be excused

to get a drink of water. Then they ran to the gym to look.

Teachers said they were going next door to borrow a book. Then they ran to the gym too.

But no one could see a thing.

By the end of the week, Mr. Bundy began to wonder what his new clothes looked like. But he was also a little worried. What if *he* couldn't see the magic cloth?

He decided to ask his assistant principal, **Ms. Moore**, to have a look. Ms. Moore was smart and quite good at her job. He was sure she would have no trouble seeing the cloth. He went straight to her office.

"I'm wondering how my new suit is coming along," said Mr. Bundy, "but I'm too busy to go check. Would you mind taking the first peek?"

"I'd be happy to," said Ms. Moore.

She hurried to the gym and knocked on the door.

"Mr. Bundy sent me to see his new clothes," she called over the noise of the **whirring** machines.

A moment later, the door opened a crack, and Ms. Moore slipped inside.

"What do you think?" asked Moe. "Have you ever seen such fine craftsmanship?"

Poor Ms. Moore! She couldn't see a thing—not a collar,

a sleeve or a button. Her head
started to spin.

Can it be that I'm a fool or unfit

for my job? she wondered. *I've tried so hard to be a good assistant principal.*

She rubbed her eyes, shook her head and looked again. But it was no use.

Ms. Moore had to think fast. If she told Moe and Ivy that she couldn't see the **outfit**, she might lose her job.

"It's . . . it's beautiful!" she said. "I'm going to tell Mr. Bundy right now how much I like his special new clothes."

She hurried to Mr. Bundy's office.

"Your suit is fabulous! I've never seen anything like it," she said.

"Really? Can you tell me about it?" he asked.

"Sorry," she said. "I've got to run and make a phone call. Bye!"

She rushed off before Mr. Bundy could ask any more questions.

3

Second Peek

Now Mr. Bundy was more curious than ever.

Roger, one of the school's top students, happened to be passing by his office. If Roger couldn't see the suit, nobody could.

"Say, Roger!" called Mr. Bundy. "Do me a favor and find out how my new suit is coming along."

Roger couldn't believe his ears.

"Sure thing, Mr. B!" he said.

Wow! he thought. *I'll be the first kid to see the principal's new clothes!*

He raced off to the gym.

The door was still open, so Roger peeked inside. He could see Moe and Ivy at their sewing machines. He leaned in to get a better look.

Moe's and Ivy's hands were moving, but Roger didn't see anything in them. Not a button. **Not a thread!**

Oh no, Roger thought. *If **Mrs. Feeny** finds out I can't see the cloth, she'll think I'm a **ninny**. She'll fail me for sure.*

On the way back to his class-
room, Roger poked his head into
Mr. Bundy's office.

"Super suit!" he said.

"Come in and tell me what it looks like," said Mr. Bundy.

"Sorry, I can't stop now," said Roger. "Mrs. Feeny is giving a spelling test, and I wouldn't want to miss it."

Mr. Bundy couldn't stand the mystery any longer.

I'll just have to go see for myself, he thought.

4

Uh-Oh

Mr. Bundy marched down the hall and walked into the gym.

He couldn't wait to see his superfabulous new suit.

"Ahem! Ahem!" He cleared

his throat loudly to let the tailors know he was there.

Moe and Ivy popped up with big smiles.

Uh-oh. Mr. Bundy thought his eyes must be tricking him. Where was his new suit? He saw *nothing*.

He blinked once.

He blinked twice.

He began to **tremble**.

How can this be? he wondered. *Am I really not good at my job? Am I really a nincompoop?*

"Is anything wrong?" asked Ivy.

"Of course not!" said Mr. Bundy. He was sure his eyes would start working again any minute. "The suit is, well . . . it's . . . fantastic! I can hardly wait to try it on."

Mr. Bundy handed Moe and
Ivy two gold stars to show how

 much he liked his new
suit.

 "I'd like to wear it to
the assembly tomorrow,"
he said. "But I guess it
won't be ready. . . ."

"Yes, it will!" said Moe. "We'll
work till it's finished and bring it
to your house in the morning."

That night, Mr. Bundy dreamed
cold and **drafty** dreams.

5

Cool Duds!

Early the next day, Moe and Ivy appeared at Mr. Bundy's front door. It seemed Mr. Bundy's eyes still weren't working because all he could see were two empty hangers held high in the air.

"Please come in," he said, trying to act as if nothing was wrong.

He led them to his living room. Ivy noticed a huge mirror on the wall.

"Excellent!" she said. "You'll get the full view of how great you look."

She stepped out of the room to give Mr. Bundy **privacy** while Moe helped him get dressed.

"You must be careful stepping into the pants," said Moe. "This cloth is very **delicate**."

"Doesn't the **fabric** feel wonderfully light and airy?" called Ivy. "It's almost like having nothing on at all, isn't it?"

Mr. Bundy stared at himself in the mirror. Staring back at him was his worried self with no suit in sight.

I hope everyone is smarter and better at their jobs than me, thought Mr. Bundy. *If not, the whole world will see me in my underwear!*

"What do you say?" asked

Moe. "Cool **duds**, right?"

"Cool? Um, ah, well, yes, very," **stammered** Mr. Bundy.

"You're all ready to go," said Moe.

"Will you be coming to the assembly?" Mr. Bundy asked.

"Thanks, but no thanks," Ivy said. "We have a bus to catch. And now, if you could pay us, we'll just run along."

Moe handed Mr. Bundy the bill. Mr. Bundy handed Moe a big bundle of money.

6

Um ... Um ...

Mr. Bundy jumped onto his bike to head for school. He couldn't help noticing how smooth and cool the metal of the bike felt on his legs.

Moe had said the cloth was very delicate. I guess that's why I'm feeling a bit chilly in my fine new suit, thought Mr. Bundy.

He quickly pedaled off to Benny's Bean House for his morning cup of coffee. He was **Benny**'s first customer.

"Good morning, Mr. . . . um . . . um . . ."

Benny couldn't finish his sentence. He was too surprised seeing what Mr. Bundy was wearing. Or wasn't wearing!

He knew some schools had a Pajama Day and wondered if

PS 88 was having an Underwear Day. Benny decided to start over and said, **"Good morning!** Coffee with plenty of milk, coming right up."

And maybe you'd like a shirt and pants to go with it, he thought.

But of course Benny didn't say that. He just filled Mr. Bundy's  cup, accepted his money and wished him a very good day.

"Thank you, Benny," said Mr. Bundy.

He had hoped Benny would **compliment** his new suit, but it was early morning and he knew Benny was a busy man.

Mr. Bundy sat outside to drink his coffee, then he hopped on his bike and went on his way. He noticed his neighbors looking a little puzzled. But they each waved and said hello, with big smiles on their faces.

7

Looking Good!

When Mr. Bundy walked into the auditorium, he saw heads turning. As he went down the aisle, he heard whispers all around him.

I hope they're saying how much

they like my new clothes, thought Mr. Bundy.

But that's not what they were saying at all.

"I think he forgot something," said **Hector**, with a chuckle.

"Oops," said Roger.

"I can't believe this," said **Nancy**.

The auditorium was buzzing. Suddenly, **Alice**, a kindergartener, called out, **"Our principal's in his underwear!"**

That did it! Everyone burst out

laughing. The truth had finally been told.

Mr. Bundy and the teachers and students **realized** they had been tricked. No one—not in the school or the town—had been willing to tell the truth because they were worried about what others would think of them.

Mr. Bundy stood on stage, red in the face, knees shaking from the chill.

But not for long.

The kids and teachers wanted to help their principal. They began passing up shirts and sweatpants, jackets and ties and caps.

"Thank you, everyone!" called Mr. Bundy.

He couldn't decide which great clothes to put on first.

Hmm, should I wear this funny bunny tie? he thought. **Sure!** *I really like these pants. And these shorts. Ooh, I love caps!*

Mr. Bundy piled on the clothes, and soon he had a brand-new super suit.

"Looking good, Mr. B!" called Roger.

Mr. Bundy invited Alice up onto the stage.

"Thank you for being so honest," he said.

He shook Alice's hand and gave her a gold star.

Everyone cheered. They knew their principal was smart and good at his job.

And they all agreed that Mr. Bundy was still the sharpest dresser in town.

Word List

aisle (I'LL): A walkway between rows of seats

auditorium (aw·d·TOR·ee·um): A large room or hall with seats

compliment (COM·pli·ment): To say something nice about something or someone

delicate (DE·li·kit): Very fine and easily hurt or torn

drafty (DRAF·tee): With cold air moving through a space

duds (DUDS): Clothes

fabric (FA·brik): Cloth

nincompoop (NIN·come·poop): A foolish person

ninny (NIN·nee): A foolish person

outfit (OUT·fit): A set of clothes

privacy (PRY·va·see): Being in a place without other people

realized (REE·uh·lized): Understood clearly

spiffy (SPI·fee): Well-dressed and stylish

stammered (STAM·merd): Stumbled over words

tailors (TAY·lers): People who make clothes fit just right

tremble (TREM·bull): To shake from nerves or excitement

tricksters (TRIK·sters): People who fool others on purpose

whirring (WURR·ing): Making a low and continuous buzzing sound

Questions

1. Do you ever worry about what others think of you? If so, when was the last time you did?

2. How do you feel about the tricksters Moe and Ivy?

3. Would you have told the truth as Alice did?

4. What piece of clothing would you have passed up to Mr. Bundy?

5. This story is based on the folktale *The Emperor's New*

Clothes. Can you name three ways this story is the same and three ways it's different from the folktale?

6. Do you agree that Mr. Bundy was "Looking good!" at the end of the story? Can you draw some cool clothes for him?

CHUCKLE YOUR WAY THROUGH THESE EASY-TO-READ ILLUSTRATED CHAPTER BOOKS!